Dr. Andrew Liddle has published widely, textbooks, articles and reviews, genre fiction, poetry and self-help manuals. An academic by training, awarded a Ph.D. for a thesis on Robert Burns, he has spent much of his working life teaching English literature. His broader interests include most contact sports, New Orleans jazz, Italian opera and the Spanish language. He was born in Halifax, Yorkshire, England, a couple of miles away from the Pennine village of Heptonstall, where Ted Hughes grew up and Sylvia Plath was buried.

BRAG OF MY HEART
The last hours of Sylvia Plath

Andrew Liddle

Published by Ofrezco Press

Copyright © 2017 Andrew Liddle

All rights reserved. This book or any portion thereof may not be reproduced or used in any manner whatsoever without the express written permission of the publisher except for the use of brief quotations in a book review.

This is a work of fiction, the product of the author's imagination. Names, characters, businesses, events, places and incidents have been used in a fictitious manner.

Author's Note

How **Sylvia Plath** spent her last night on earth and what drove her to suicide, while her children were sleeping soundly, will never be known. ***Brag Of My Heart*** is a sympathetic and imaginative exploration of her final hours. It captures her mental turmoil, vividly, as she battles her demons, reliving the best and worst of times while communing with herself, her parents and her estranged husband, **Ted Hughes.** Drawing on her poetry and journals for insight into the creative chaos of her mind, her mood swings and self-loathing, it is above all an original interpretation of what might have occurred and a dramatic – at times terrifying – scream of consciousness.

Sylvia gassed herself in the early hours of the 11th of February, 1963, having made sure her two children, Frieda and Nicholas, were safe, by sealing off their room. She had made several previous attempts on her life, the first of which may well have been about a decade earlier, in August, 1953, when she overdosed on pills at her mother's home. Her most recent was probably in June, 1962, when she drove her car into a river, later admitting to the police it had been a deliberate act.

At the time of her death, she was being treated for clinical depression by Dr. John Horder, who had recently prescribed the antidepressant, *monoamine oxidase,* and arranged for her to have a live-in nurse. Sylvia committed suicide at around 4.30 in the morning and the nurse duly arrived at nine o'clock, too late, alas, to save her from carbon monoxide poison. Suggestions that Sylvia might have hoped to be revived have been discussed by several writers, based on tenuous evidence. We will never precisely know the truth.

This is a novella, not a work of biography, and its *raison d'etre* is to imaginatively create the emotions of the last hours of the tortured genius, not to add to the confusion of the precise circumstances of her death. Readers who take an interest in literary biography may, however, be interested to learn, in the epilogue, what happened to the other characters named and the tragic self-destructive thread that runs through the extended narrative.

It is, of course, wholly impossible to even begin to guess what might go through a vulnerable person's mind in the build-up to ending everything. I have had, necessarily, to make certain assumptions about what Sylvia would think about, and to use certain stylistic and narrative devices to convey these thoughts. The text is elliptical, broken into segments, a device to both suggest the passage of time and the silent *longueurs* between the moments of lucidity and mental agitation.

One is entitled to a degree of certainty that Sylvia would reflect on her past, her previous suicide attempts, perhaps, the people close to her and on her supreme talent as a poet. She might well choose not to dwell on the fate of her children, such the enormity of her decision to abandon them.

We would expect her to vacillate between extremes of emotion, hope and despair, doubt and certainty, hesitation and resolution. Knowing her as we do, we should prepare ourselves for a quantity of black humour, of the kind expressed in, say, *Lady Lazarus*, her poem about suicide being attempted.

The inner voice that we hear ranges from fragmentary utterance to expressions of some magniloquence. To a large extent I have attempted the impossible in having Sylvia 'speak' at moments of high emotion in the style of her own poetry. Occasionally, I play safe and borrow from her writings (sometimes she quotes herself) but where I have used my own poetic skills, the reader must accept that no one could come near to her powers of expression.

I have, at all times, tried to reflect Sylvia's love of life as well as her deep anxieties. Ultimately, she lost the battle that raged within her and pathos proliferates even if there are moments of levity and, increasingly, the self-effacing humour of the condemned person. I found myself shedding tears whilst writing it and you must steel yourself for an explosion of catharsis as you turn the last page, even though the outcome can never have been in doubt.

BRAG OF MY HEART
The last hours of Sylvia Plath

Ring telephone ring! Let me hear you sing. Will not somebody telephone me?

No, then I'll answer it anyway. Helloooooooo! Anybody there?

Nobody there. Nobody wants to speak to Sylvia? None of my erstwhile Cambridge friends? No literary types? Maybe Sylvia does not care to talk to them.

So, it's you and me, then … dear journal, keeper of my private thoughts, sharer of my most intimate secrets, my *vade-mecum*. Let me see what gems I can find lurking within to while away the watches of the night.

God what a mess! How is anybody supposed to read this?

'I desire the things that will destroy me in the end …'

Did I write that? Did I mean that?

Sometimes I feel as if I ought to just pick up this telephone and dial numbers at random. I have a fervent wish to speak to somebody, tonight … anybody … who might not want to tyrannise me.

'I feel outcast under a cold star, unable to feel anything but an awful helpless numbness.' How true, Sylvie. How true.

Come on and fucking ring, can't you!

Just ring! *Ting-a-ling, ting-a-ling.* I dare you to?

Hello, is there anyone there?

Temper, temper, Sylvia! No good taking it out on the poor old receiver, slamming it down like that. If you're not careful you'll break it then nobody will ever get through to you.

Well, if they do not want to speak me, I surely do not want to speak to them.

'A passionate, fragmentary girl, maybe.'

That's me, hey? Maybe? There's no maybe about it. And these jottings are the fragments of my soul.

They do not want to know me now, you know. Now that I'm no longer with Mr. H.

From what grace am I fallen!

Let me begin an entry for today. I think I'll start with the date, what better way? It's still February, I know that. I can tell it by the cold seeping through the windows, just as it has done all interminable winter long. No wonder I've had flu for as long as I can remember, sneezing wet and soggy, piling up sodden frayed Kleenex tissues, throat aching, eyes twitching …

It's the tenth, unless I miss my guess. No, midnight's chimes have sounded. It must be the eleventh. The eleventh of February, 1963. Strange how each new day breaks at midnight, not at daybreak.

At midnight when demons are most active. No one disturbs them here but the caustic ticking of the clock, cicada-loud whenever I try to hear my deepest thoughts.

I sit alone, swaddled in a dressing gown and a blanket that reeks of vomit, in this squalid little room of my squalid little flat, in the ironically named Primrose Hill, where of dalliance there is none.

And nothing better to divert my attention than ... this mute telephone ... these mouldering journals ... this bottle of pills ... this mirror ... and, oh yes, a baby bottle in need of a refill.

In my mind I think I've always had him down as Mr. H. I cannot now bring myself to call his name.

H is for him.

H is for horrible.

H is for hell.

H is for hack - a mediocre jobbing writer who is professionally successful. A writer for hire putting other people's thoughts into words he's borrowed from somebody else. Yes 'Mr. H' is about right for him, the J. Arthur Ranker!

Forgive me if I am laughing vulgarly.

No, not that, silly ... let's not forget that Mr H was 'Senior Reader' for J. Arthur Rank, that's how he described himself with some degree of unpardonable pride, I would say, when trying to impress me with his ten pounds a week and prospects of twelve. Mr. H, the father of my two children. Mr. H who shared my bed ... and other beds.

A man whom we might say nibbled more than the occasional bonbon of sin.

But what did he see in that woman, that Assia? Assia, the assassin. Assia, the assimilator. Assia who escaped the incinerator.

Assia who tried to pass herself off as a man and never wanted kids in case she might lose her figure! 'She would rather be dead than fat, dead and perfect, like Nefertit …'

Well, she's got one now, so I hear.

He's given her one.

She certainly usurped my position in the unholy court at Court Green, where rumour has it she is now queen.

If I could remember her number I'd give her a congratulatory call, since she's not going to ever phone me to share the good news. No one ever rings. If you expect nothing from somebody you are never disappointed. *Ah!*

And say what? 'Hi, Ass, great news about the baby!'

Maybe not. She didn't exactly give me too much encouragement last time we spoke.

But what the hell, I will give her a call, anyway. Who cares? I'm past caring, past worrying about other people's feelings. Past even worrying about my own.

Ring, telephone, ring.

'Assia Wevill speaking.'

I guess I'd better deepen the voice to be her, although I could never manage to catch that delicious note of surprise and breathy caution that came over her when she heard me on the line.

'Assia Wevill speaking. Er, I mean, this is a friend of Ted's.'

Is that a woman there?

'Er, no I'm not a woman, er, I'm a man, er, just here to … '

To what, Assia?

To minister to his ego and to see to his other needs, perhaps.

He wouldn't like what I've been writing about him recently, you know. He wouldn't be talking any more about us getting back together, not that he ever actually means that. He's just like that. Never wants to let go. He likes to keep all his options open, especially where women are concerned. He likes to have lots of sleeping partners.

He'd want to destroy my words, obliterate them. So would she.

℘

It must be a blessing to be able to sleep. I'd give anything to be able to sleep soundly at night. To sleep fitfully would be very heaven. To sleep at all is something devoutly to be wished.

Care-charmer sleep could you not ravish me this very moment? I would gladly surrender myself to you, kind sir. Take me, take me!

All right then don't; please yourself!

Sometimes I wonder if we, the vigilant ones who brave the perils of the night, do sleep more than we know. Do we occasionally nod off, drift in and out of dormancy? Have periods of unconsciousness so vivid we imagine we are awake? It would not greatly surprise me, given the pills I pop and the booze and all, but if I am asleep more than I know then I am dreaming more than I know - and how amazingly sad to have such ... phantasmagoric reveries.

Watch-keeping by day is certainly much less harrowing, if not as fecund, poetically.

※

There goes the clock again, striking one, breaking the silence of silence with its long-drawn-out whine.

One o'clock is such a mournful sound, I always say, a solitary shriek with nothing to reinforce it. I hear it night after night, round about this time.

One night is pretty much like any other, an eternity in a dark maze, from which you only emerge at first light.

Give me the clamour of midnight, any time. Midnight that gives promise of the long day-night ahead turning out interesting for once. One o'clock brings the rude awakening! The night is come and nothing is going to happen.

Maybe, just maybe, this night will turn out different. What d'ya think, Sylv?

I burned his manuscripts, made a bonfire of them, compounded them with the filthy parings of his cruel fingernails and the detritus of his skull, the dessicated dandruff he scattered on his desk. No man ever had dandruff like he did, you know.

Never washed his hair. Never. He was much too macho to wash his hair, was Ted.

I feel disgusted to have such thoughts. To have been married to such a man disgusts me now. That's me, I guess, 'Disgusted of Primrose Hill'! I think I should write to the *Telegraph* about him.

I read them first then burned them and incanted over them like a witch. I learned all that spooky baloney from him, you know. He believed it all and his family swore by it. He couldn't write his stuff without invoking it all. He forced it on me, bought me Tarot cards and that bloody ouija board. There was a time we were gonna be rich, win the football pools by consulting the oracle.

He was a complete fantasist, as hollow as a soundbox ... but I believed him, at the time, went along with him, allowed his personality to dominate mine.

He always wanted to somehow cheat his way, fluke his way, blag his way to the plaudits. 'We must study the stars, Sylv, we must study the stars,' he used to say.

He was married to one, the asshole, but didn't know it.

I wonder if I can still do his Yorkshire accent. 'Is there anybody there? Knock three times if there is!'

'Oh Ted, this is all nonsense. Let's stop. Let's go for a walk.'

'Is there someone there? Make yourself known if there is.'

'Ted!'

'No, c'mon, Sylv, give it a chance. There might be somebody there.'

'There's no one there, Ted. There ain't no one there!'

There never was. There never is! Nothing's changed!

If there is, don't bother knocking, just c'mon in … or, say, just give me a call, big boy. Sylvia's waiting. *Come up and see me sometime.*

It ain't gonna ring. I have a presentiment it will never ring again.

It was weird. I watched the flames, choked on the smoke, as his words turned to ashes and then, suddenly … this teeny-tiny scrap just curled upwards and glided down, slowly, slowly, slowly, and settled on my foot. And I was shaking as I read the single word.

It was 'Assia'. I kid you not, it was 'Assia'!

It fell on me like a curse. It made me shake with pity and terror. It was the strangest most godawful feeling I ever felt. And I've had some … all right.

I heard that silly play of his on the radio last week, all about giving red roses to his mistress. What was it called … ee bah gum … *'The Difficulties of a Bridegroom'*.

Pompous ass! Fucking prig!

I don't remember him having any particular difficulties when it came to grooming this particular bride!

He told me last week … came round here to tell me in person … he's getting a solicitor to stop me. A solicitor to stop me writing. A solicitor will solicit me to stop talking.

Will Mr. H allow me to talk to his children, I wonder … or should I clothe them and feed them in silence? Maybe, I must ask the solicitor. Solicit him for permission to speak, sir!

He said to me, 'You're smoking. What are you doing that for? You've always been very much against smoking.'

'What do I care?' I said.

'They're bad for your health.'

He sounded quite concerned, funny though that might seem.

'Yes,' I said, 'I'd better look after my health. We wouldn't want that to break down. Does Assia smoke?'

'Not that Ah've noticed,' he said, sounding like one of those north country comedians that he always pretends to think are so rib-ticklingly funny! Actually, he has zero sense of humour.

'She will!' said I, in triumph.

Time is passing, slipping by like inky water. But still I can't sleep. I feel like a wild beast, a shadowy thing I can't quite see or put a name to, is stalking me. My heart is beating fast, my face flaring. I guess I'm having what they call a panic attack. I feel the need to pace about.

Calm down, take deep breaths, Sylv. I could do with a smoke.

But I've run out. I went down to Prof Thomas's a while back and borrowed some stamps from him. I've got letters to write. I said, 'I'm fresh out of *Lucky Strikes* tonight', but he didn't seem to get it. Didn't think it was kinda funny.

I can't remember what exactly he's a professor of or what, indeed, he professes. He's a kindly old soul, my guess is, but not the brightest.

So I asked him for a cigarette, came straight out with it and he said, 'You shouldn't be smoking, Sylvia, they're extremely bad for your health.'

I mean ... how about that? *My health*.

Why is everybody so goddamn concerned about *my* health? Do they know something?

I wonder if he thought I looked a little odd, a little *distraite,* perhaps ... like a mad woman about to do something desperate. It's possible he might decide to, er, ring somebody. It wouldn't surprise me ... if I were thwarted again. It would not be the first time.

They tell me she's a poet – and German-born! One who survived!

How about *that*!

Assia Gutmann she was called when I first knew her. We Jews know all about gas ovens, do we not!

※

What it's like in New England now, I'd love to know, Mommy? It can't be as cold as London. London is as cold as death. I would probably never have left Devon but for the Assassin!

*'In a leafy lane of Devon
There's a cottage that I know,
Then a garden - then, a grey old crumbling wall,
And the wall's the wall of heaven ...'*

You see, you see, I can remember other poets' lines, Ted. I'm not just about myself. Strangely, I can never remember any of *your* lines, Ted. Only the ones you stole from me.

I don't need water to swallow pills, you know. I'm pretty adept at tossing them back. It's easy, really, if you just take a handful, throw them at the back of your throat and gulp and gobble, gobble, gobble like a turkey.

I've taken a pill to kill ...

I wonder if these pills are killing me? Dr. Horder, Dr Horder, what kind of a name is that? Dr. H are you in confederation with your namesake, Mr. H?

There was a medical man called Horder, who gave me some pills in order ... to add balm to my soul ... and make me feel whole ... but they only worsened my manic disorder.

Well, my, my! How about that for an extempore effusion! It rhymes even if it does not quite scan, I suppose. I've never written a limerick before. I think I must be cracking up! I'll be writing like bloody Wordsworth next. Let me try another.

I wandered lonely as a cloud ... er ... that's floating high and proud, searching till I found Ted, busy a-scratching his head ... while through the thesaurus he ploughed.

Oh yes, that is really very funny, Sylv, go ahead and laugh. You have such a surprising knack for this kind of stuff. Some might call it gallows' humour.

Dr. Nolan would have known. Dr. Nolan would not have prescribed pills. Dr. Nolan knew best.

You know, she blamed my mom for everything. Well, I mean Esther's mom, not my mom. I'd better make that clear. Let me set that down in the journal. Esther Greenwood, I'm talking about, not me.

You know Mom's name on the distaff side was Grünwald! I really don't know why I'm giggling at that.

Some say my poems do not scan. They scan for me when I say them, when I hear them, in my head.

'A grey wall now, clawed and bloody.
Is there no way out of the mind?
Steps at my back spiral into a well.
There are no trees or birds in this world,
There is only sourness.'

I think I called that one 'Apprehensions'. What a dumb word!

Why have we got to have apprehensions? Strange how that word has somehow, kinda, moved from understanding and perception to my kind of anxiety. Johnny Panic. Maybe without perception there is no anxiety. Maybe without anxiety there is no perception. And without anxiety there is no poetry.

※

What does Ted know about my feelings? He's too obsessed with his own.

'The falcon who spoke clear to Canacee cries gibberish to coarsened ears.'

It was from whispering, riddling sources that I heard about his falsehoods. I would not have believed any other source. That man was born to cheat. Thought it made him a poet. The truest poets are the most feigning was one of his sayings.

Perhaps I'll essay another limerick. Let's take solace where we may.

Dr. Nolan, oh good Dr Nolan, some of your fame I have stolen. When The Bell Jar I wrote, it was you I did quote - and with your ideas was I swollen.

I really think limericks could be sort of fun, you know, the complete antidote to, shall we say, Hughesian pretentiousness. I wonder if there's a career in it for me. Of course I wouldn't publish them under my own name.

Edwina Clare might be a good name. Or maybe Naomi Weiss sounds better, is more in keeping. More kosher. Let me give it some thought. One of my most astonishing discoveries is the power of names. I'm really very good at thinking them up and making up a life for them.

Don't like that last line much, though. Maybe it should be - let me say it portentously - 'I took what you said as an *omen*!'

Yes, that's better, very much better. There's nothing quite like a good omen, is there! You know where you are with an omen, don't you! Something bad is bound to ensue. That's the way it works. I'll say Omen to that!

I've done it before, you know. Ten years ago. One year in every ten I manage it.

And more frequently recently! Always a botch. The bitch botch!

Botch! Botch! Botch! Perhaps I wasn't as fearless as I should have been, who knows.

That is something I would have liked to teach my children, to be fearless.

There's hardly any pills left in this bottle, this time, not enough to paralyse a stunted flee. Not enough to anaesthetise an ant sounds better. Not enough a quietus to make. Only enough for another fucking flubbing foul-up.

I wouldn't use pills this time. I would do the job properly, if I did it at all. You know, if I wanted to achieve stasis in darkness and all that, as the poet said, euphemistically. I wouldn't want to go through that again.

I shudder at the thought. It must have been a pretty gross spectacle.

Being wired up and having all that electricity going round inside the brain. It can't be good for you. Stop laughing, Sylvia, that's not funny. Let's be serious for a moment.

I said, 'Stop laughing!'

Sometimes I wonder if it was that which made me the poet I am. Acted like a psychoactive drug in the brain, changed all the wiring, you know. Opened up new channels, turned over stones and let creative creepy-crawly things come skulking out.

I wonder what Ted would say to that. He'd think it had given *me* an unfair advantage and he'd want *his* brain wired up – so he could write proper poetry. He would, you know.

He just would. I know him so well.

He's tried everything else to improve himself. Very big on self-hypnotism, he is.

All that deep breathing, that pallid and perfunctory stream-of-consciousness concentration on the object stuff - and then, hey *prestissimo*, out pops his latest, always the greatest, arcane masterpiece.

Trouble is … it's the very reverse of what he thinks it is. He's painting by numbers, sticking in a simile here, an oxymoron there to order. His sustained fucking metaphors that he's fiercely proud of are so mechanically contrived, somehow. I know because I've seen him do it.

He's nothing but a learned casuist, a poetising polemicist, never prone to knowingly understate his case. Not Ted!

I couldn't bear to write like that. I couldn't live with myself.

D'you know, he used to brood resentfully for hours and hours when he knew I'd effortlessly tossed off in an hour something better than he could ever labour over in a month of saturdays and sundays?

He'd be outraged. Horrified. Disgusted with me, as though it was somehow my fault.

Actually, I took his jealous moods as an inspiration to write. I fed off his soul's malefic disorders. He never knew that, or he'd have effused an ineffable sweetness and euphoria around me. Yes he would. Don't think he wouldn't. He was capable of anything. Even of being nice when it suited his purpose.

Then he'd start that bloody off-key whistling, each foul breath intimidating like the swish of a sword. He knew that sound was so precious to me and I couldn't stand his godawful whistling. That's why he did it. Kept it up for hours. It was torture, worse than fingernails on a blackboard.

The funny thing is … the more grudging and bitchy he was, the better I wrote. It's true and it makes perfectly good sense, actually, when I think about it.

There goes the two. Right on time. Comes around like clockwork, same time every night, never a minute late, a minute early.

I was expecting it. It's become an old friend lately.

You could set your clock by it.

I shouldn't laugh at that, it's not that funny. Lots of people wouldn't find it funny at all.

Two is much better than one.

I shall never grow old. That is a mercy. That is the joy of death.

Let me count the corny old blessings, *name them one by one*. I shall never have … corns, arthritis, rheumatism, stomach ulcers, a stroke … or cursed gangrene, will I!

I shall be the dead lion to his living dog!

※

You came over last summer, Mommy. Didn't stay long. Said you were coming to see Nicholas but I know you were checking me out.

Check! Check! Check!
Peck! Peck! Peck!
Dreck! Dreck! Dreck!

That was always the problem with you, Mom. You always had to check and double-check on everyone and everything, specially me. You made everyone feel nervous, somehow, with your infernal stridulations. I guess you never stopped being the school teacher.

Little things, like high school grades, meant so much to you, and who was dating whom in Wellesley and the ins and outs of Smith College. Your appetite was insatiable for these things. You wanted me to share your interests, your secrets, be in your image. And I could never be - and so I could never please you, Mommy.

Little Sylv could never please Big Momma.

When Sylv was good, she was very, very good! But when she was bad ... she was rotten. Wasn't she, Momma?

I said some bad things about you in my book. True things but bad things. I know they'd hurt you if you ever got to read them which is why I told Heinemann to call me ... ssshhh, let me whisper it ... Victoria Lucas.

Good name that, hey! A luminous name. A numinous name. A good name for somebody who got a *Fulbright* scholarship, don't you think!

My mother's name, Aurelia, means gold.

You know, Mommy, how you were always bragging about how you had graduated second in your high school class. That means you were silver not gold.

I never told you but I think I'd sooner have come last than second. Who wants to come second in anything! Who wants to be a second-rater? I should imagine Ted would settle for that, aspire to it even.

He'd settle for the second tier of the literary pantheon. Not me! Not Sylvia!

And then at Boston University, Mommy, you were the *valedictorian*! Wow! How many times did I hear that? When I was a little girl I used to wonder what that meant. It meant you were so good you got to give a little speech at graduation. I can see you now standing there on the platform, all dressed up, made up, hair in a lacquered bundle, smiling around, feigning nerves and loving every last moment of it.

I can see it as clearly as if I had been there. I just know. I have this second sight, you see. Always have had. I think I'm cursed with it.

I think on this night of nights I am, perhaps, the real valedictorian, Mommy!

※

You remember when I was ten years old, Mom, and you sent me off to Camp, on Lake Ossipee, in leafy, leafy New Hampshire?

Lake Ossipee! Now that's a name for you, ain't it! Sounds like a quantity of equine urine!

That's not *that* funny, Sylvia. Let's not get silly again.

A big puddle for the sun to gild! Lake Ossipee, I love you!

You were poorly *again* - poor you - so I was packed off. Packed off to camp, like any all-American gal. Gee!

I certainly had the right hair colour for the role at that time. I certainly made up for the role, played up to the role, youthful breasts full of champagne, nippled with caviar. Eager beaver! Oh yes!

I don't think I was ever happier. It was the one and only time I had both freedom and purpose to my life. Write that down, Sylvia. Underline it! Remember it. Let them see it.

Each day I awoke with the sun coming up to the rousing plangent sound of the bugle, *ta-ran-ta-ran-ta-ran-tara,* and the piney, briney tang of the lake. I wish it could have gone on forever.

I think I begin to feel another bilious little limerick coming on.

When I was in Lake Ossipee, I forgot all about philosophy, I awoke with the sun, had a mountain of fun, and never spoke of … pathology … neurology … lobotomy … atrocity?

Which is it?

Clearly needs working on. Maybe tomorrow.

There's nothing to compare with waking up naturally, is there, and then going for a swim, working up an appetite, catching your breakfast in the water - and struggling to light the tiny gas stove to boil some water.

Isn't that what life should be about? Simple and innocent and everything that my present life is not. It's difficult, if not impossible from this distance, to explain the tremulous joy of those days on the lake.

Gone now, gone forever. Forever fled!

But let's not cry, Sylv. There's no one here to see us. What is the point of weeping when one is weeping alone? It's just a waste of precious tears.

I think I actually feel a real poem coming on. Sylvia might say the lake was her *omphalos* and …

What a pity it may never be written. Better not let the idea of a poem get in the way of life's real drama.

Everything that summer was about the lake.

We swam in it … fished in … fossicked foolishly in it … sailed on it and tramped around it, picking blackberries on the go. They tasted divine, as we freaked out, tripping on fresh air and giving each other bear hugs.

I remember a white-tailed eagle soaring majestically, and suddenly plummeting. *Ah me!*

And we had to read these improving books about great American heroes and make things with our hands. At night the bursting stars seemed so close you could almost reach out and touch them. Oh boy!

Girls made sighs and boys, ritual promises. Everybody was passing little notes to everybody else.

One night we watched *Casablanca* and I fell in love with Rick.

The world was wonderful, truly wonderful. If only life could always be that wholesome – that pure and simple and fresh.

Fresh like the virgin's dream of her first kiss - under moonlight and stars.

※

I know this is going to sound kinda crazy but it says here, 'Ted is my salvation. He is so rare, so special, how could anyone else stand me!'

You know, Sylvie, you must have really gone for that Ted of yours. I've got to ask, where did it all go wrong?

Don't ask! Just don't ask!

I seriously question if this phone is ever going to ring again. I figure there'll have to be the occasional wrong number. That kind of thing is bound to happen once in a while.

But not tonight. Tonight is not the kind of night for wrong numbers, serendipity pleasures, chance encounters or any weary traveller to come knocking at my door. Tonight is a lonely beast, a secret, slant-wise, silent creature.

But wait! What is this? Do I hearken to the sound of the bell? Huh?

Hello, who's calling? Are you a wrong number? Oh it's Buddy Willard on the line, hey?

Not Buddy Willard, well then it must be Buddy

Somebodyelse. Hiya Buddy, how ya gettin' on? How was camp? How's the folks back home? You couldn't lend me a smoke, couldya?' Buddy can yer spare a … smoke?

Well, would you believe it, Buddy's kinda rung off! Some buddy he was.

※

We met in Cambridge, Mr. H and me. I know him now to be a little man, a *little* little man but there was a time when he meant all the world to me. He loved me then, that big, dark, hunky boy, the only one there huge enough for me. I thought he looked kind of like Kirk Douglas without the dimple.

Threw stones at my window, the naughty boy, which hit me in the heart. It was about this time in the morning then … and it's still about that time now, so many years later. Ain't life strange! What a coincidence!

I'm in bed with this other guy and, suddenly, this clown is throwing stones at us. And best of all, he's throwing them at the wrong fucking window!

I mean you gotta laugh … to keep from crying.

We met at a party. It was like one of those *jejune* things you read about in drippy magazines. I walked in the room and saw him and forgot about the guy I was with. What *was* that guy's name?

Hamish, I think. Yeah, Hamish Stewart. With a name like that he would have to like his whiskey, I guess, and we'd been pouring it down us all night. We walked into this crowded place full of every poet in town and their saintly Botolophian fellow-travellers, pimply verse-makers, rhymesters and Bohemian ballad-mongers.

Everyone was drunk or so it seems when you are, the air was full of jazz and cigarette smoke and, strangely, all I could see was this lovely dangerous man with a boxer's jaw and shoulders like wedges, like he'd got a coat hanger under his coat. He was all over the women, a blonde one in particular.

He liked blondes. Maybe I should have been, like, a red-head!

What was it Lester was playing, soft and low? *Mean To Me.* Yes that was it.

'Mean to me, why must you always be mean to me, gee honey, don't you know what you mean to me?'

A tune to haunt and how impossibly right for the soundtrack of the occasion. Part of life's rich … pantomime.

If you look at somebody long enough, some instinct tells them. Suddenly he turned and saw me, I knew he was going to, and I knew he was going to come over to me.

He trod warily at first and kind of circled. What was it I wrote about him: 'There is a panther stalks me down; one day I'll have my death of him.'

He was trying to weigh me up. He wanted to see me

as this pretty young girl he could conquer at will but in his mind he was sensing my darker side, my strangeness. I know he was. Maybe that's what attracted him.

I bit his cheek, made the blood pour. We Jews like to retaliate first. That was after he told me he had 'obligations', in the next room. What a thing to say! *Obligations!* Obligations turned out to be a short piece in a short skirt, showing her stocking-tops, called Shirley.

Then he ripped off my headband, wow, that red one I always did like, probably thinking he was making some great symbolic gesture, and kissed me full on the lips. Wowee! Like big wow!

That should get it, he was thinking. That should make a statement. She'll be putty in my hands now.

I think he saw himself as some kind of priapic Orpheus in a Humphrey Bogart trilby!

Humphrey! Did I say 'Humphrey'? What kind of a name is that for a great lover, like Rick?

Edward James Hughes, what kind of a name is that for anything except a Puritan. It has about as much warmth to it as Uriah the Hittite. About as much warmth as the bus-driver grey suit he was wearing. Grey was always his colour.

I remember thinking he had deep wrinkles in his forehead for a man of his age, as if he spent too much time frowning or looking at himself in the mirror. And flecks of dandruff on his collar, abundant as … snowflakes in Siberia!

They didn't bother me that much at the time. I just chose to ignore them, I guess. Can't pretend I didn't see them. No one, except him, could have missed them.

Excuse me, Sylvia, while I just make a note of my feelings of repugnance. I can't let this moment pass without placing it on record.

We went on honeymoon in Spain, you know. Benidorm.

Dormire bene! Who does that on honeymoon!

※

Most of all I remember the heat and the passion. The vibrance of the colours. The red watermelon sun.

And above everything, the vibrance of the noise comes back to me now. 'The lovers hear loudspeakers boom, from each neon-lit palm rumbas and sambas no ear-flaps can muffle.' That was certainly true, although not a problem. It added to the excitement.

We were happy then. For a while. If happiness ever really exists, is anything more than a cruel chimera, a blood clot on the impatient heart.

I wonder if I remember it right? The journals never lie. Let me see. Ah here it is: Sunday morning, July 22nd, 1956. 'Our new house is magnificent …'

So it was. 'Never did a new bride queen it over her deep-freeze, washing machine, pressure cooker, *et al* … as I do over my one-ring petrol stove.'

What's this I wrote about Ted: 'His mind is the biggest, most imaginative, I have ever met ...'

Was it his *mind* I was talking about?

Will you look at this: 'Never in my life have I had conditions so perfect ... A magnificent handsome brilliant husband ... Perfect mental and physical wellbeing ... Each day we feel stronger, wider awake.'

Sounds like domestic bliss. Sounds like a dizzy green girl talking. Sound like the mockery triumph again. The imposter hope at it again.

It doesn't sound much like Sylvia.

It was not long before, if I remember right, that I began to experience unfathomable qualms, inward quandary, serpents at my throat.

Indeed, the very next day, July 23. 'Alone, deepening ... the hurt going in clear as a razor, and the dark blood welling. Just the sick knowing that the wrongness was growing in the full moon. Listening he scratches his chin, the small rasp of a beard. He is not asleep.'

There's pages and pages of this stuff. Ghastly, dreadful stuff.

'We sit far apart on stones and bristling dry grass. The light is cold, cruel and still. All could happen, the wilful drowning, the murder, the killing words ...'

Horrible! Horrible! Horrible! And so sudden.

Oh I don't believe this: 'Two silent strangers ... there is the growing sickness, the separate sleep, the sour waking. And all the time, the wrongness growing, creeping, choking the house, twining the tables and chairs and poisoning the knives and forks, clouding the drinking water with that lethal taint. Sun falls off-key on eyes asquint, and the world has grown crooked and sour as lemon overnight.'

The trouble is it is all true and I think it was not longer after that he tried to kill me. *I wish he had.*

He would have saved me the trouble and gone to the electric chair for his pains in sparing my pains.

I can feel his hands closing about my neck now, not being able to breathe, choking, the black bile rising.

I really thought I was going to die when he put those big fists round my throat and started to squeeze. I wasn't at all scared. I looked him, unflinching, in the eye and spat in his face.

But that's all a lifetime ago. Years have passed, anniversaries have come and gone and Christmases; children have arrived, words been spoken, have been blazoned in print, houses have been lived in and promises broken. Hearts have beaten and blood has streamed through veins towards the infinite chambers of the mind, the mazy, labyrinthine mind daily toiling to confront futility and searching for the perfect anaesthetic, the novocaine needle into the heart that powers it.

Was that really me, in Benidorm, or was it somebody else? Have I ever had perfect mental well-being? Sometimes I wonder, I really do wonder, at times, when things spiral out of control, who I might be.

Who am I? Who are you, Sylvia? What secrets do you know?

I look in the mirror and what do I see? I see a little girl with big wide eyes - lost and hunted eyes. I see somebody who is timid … and aggressive, someone who swings between the two. Someone who has great difficulty moving in society, doing the simple things like fixing beans on toast or changing my baby's diaper.

You cannot simply get on with the basic business of living, Sylvia, can you? You are hopeless at looking after yourself. The world for you is a dangerous place. You can never stop watching it with those big eyes. There is something about you that is ever vigilant, as though you were being stalked by a panther … while you are stalking it.

> *'Now I am a lake. A woman bends over me,*
> *Searching my reaches for what she really is.*
> *Then she turns to those liars, the candles or the moon.*
> *I see her back, and reflect it faithfully.*
> *She rewards me with tears and an agitation of hands.*
> *I am important to her. She comes and goes.*
> *Each morning it is her face that replaces the darkness.*
> *In me she has drowned a young girl, and in me an old woman*
> *Rises toward her day after day, like a terrible fish.'*

Ted backed me into another room, you know, the first time we met. He knew my name, even though I didn't know who he was, although I guess I already knew and admired his poetry.

He had this deep, deep voice and this comical accent, sort of manly and so unlike the suave tones of the natural Cambridge type. He didn't sound that English. I thought he was Polish at first. He wasn't but he certainly lacked *polish*! Actually, he was Heathcliff to the very life. That's who he was. Still is. Always will be. That's him in a nutshell. I don't know why I've never thought of that before.

It was not exactly the Cambridge way to tell me about his fucking obligations. It was after that that I hated him. Served him right, really, that I bit him. Obliged him with his own blood.

Why did he have to go and spoil the eternal moment with bloody obligations?

You know I can't stop thinking about it. It bugs me.

How can anyone have *obligations* at a literary party when everybody's drunk? My God, there was Lester on the gramophone, playing his heart out, and Ted had obli-fucking-gations!

Hasn't he got obligations right now to me, the mother of his two children? Or do his obligations to the Assassin countervail!

There was a poet called Wevill, whose reflections were all on one level, but when Ted saw her lines, he forgot all his rhymes, and sold his soul ... to the very Devil!

I think that's your son crying, Ted. I must go in and see him.

That's what mothers do, isn't it. That's what they're supposed to do. Especially when Daddy's not around. They say a mother can always hear her own child crying? Even if she's a thousand miles away.

Oh thank goodness, Nicholas has stopped. I was so afraid he might awake and spoil everything.

℘

Some illnesses cannot be diagnosed. Some things that are mere essences in the mind are more deadly than gangrene. A gush can kill instantly where a cancer might take months.

It's the strangest of feelings knowing that the unequal struggle may soon be over. There's an obvious fear, of course, a gnawing in the pit of the belly, like something growing and growling inside of me. It's not that I want to do it. I want to live like everybody else wants to live. It's simply I feel a sort of inevitability. Almost, dare I say it, an *obligation*!

Maybe, the day of doom is not yet come.
If not now, then tomorrow.

If not tomorrow, then maybe next week, next month, or next year. But one day soon, quite soon, we'll do it, won't we, Sylv!

There is something that lies dormant within everything that lives, waiting for the moment of implementation.

Is it a gene … shall we call it the suicide gene? … that pulls me … compels me … controls me? Or could we say I'm simply in a dark machine being ground by the indifferent millstones of circumstance?

A logical response then, Sylvia?

I shall never grow into a tense, angry, frustrated and vindictive person, Mom.

Johnny Panic will never visit me again.

'But how can there possibly be any sense in abandoning your two lovely children? You haven't thought of that, Sylvia, have you?'

What did I once write, journal? 'To annihilate the world by annihilation of one's self is the deluded height of desperate egoism. The simple way out of all the little brick dead ends we scratch our nails against … I want to kill myself, to escape from responsibility, to crawl back abjectly into the womb.'

You bet I've thought about it, Mom. I've thought about it over and over again. My palms are sweating and I am trembling at the thought of it, now. Believe me.

'How could you tuck them up in bed, Sylvia, whisper soft words to them, see that they are sleeping safe and soundly, knowing they will wake up to a motherless world that will never be the same again? What pain they will go through God only knows.'

I know, I know but I don't want to think about it. Just shut up, won't you! I'm not going to listen.

'But Sylvia, I implore you ...'

I'm not listening. I'm going to close my eyes now, Mommy, and pretend I'm asleep.

'You're behaving selfishly like you always behave, Sylvia. You always want your own way in everything and if you can't get it, you always blow up. If you don't calm down and go and do your Math homework, you'll get bad grades and Daddy and I will be very upset.'

But, Mom ... how can you call it selfish of me to make this ultimate sacrifice of the most precious thing a person possesses? It is a far far better thing - a near near thing - that I do than I have ever done before ... and all that twaddle.

'Oh isn't that just typical of you, Sylvia, avoiding reality, quoting Shakespeare when you should be concentrating on the real world. Where will that get you? Why can't you be more like other girls. I just don't know how you're gonna turn out.'

It wasn't Shakespeare, Momma, it was Dickens!

'Why can't you just appreciate the sacrifices Daddy and I are making for you? *Gornisht helfn*!'

The really crazy thing, you know, is to be sitting here, discussing it, as if there's anything to discuss. As if I haven't already made up my mind, hardened my heart, stiffened the sinews. Done all the preparation.

'What preparation, Sylvia?'

You know, sealed off the kitchen and all, so that it won't get to the children.

'If you care at all about the children, don't do it, Sylvia. Think again.'

What if I cannot go through with it?

What if Dr. Horder's nurse arrives in the morning in time to revive me. That would be fairly typical, wouldn't it? The usual botch-up. Would I be safe then for another decade till the urge comes upon me again?

Is it all a rather pathetic *cri de coeur*? That's what they always call it, isn't it. That makes it sound as though I am a someone desperate to be heard by a someone.

Are you crying out to Ted, Sylv?

I would say not.

But you'd be the last one to know, wouldn't you?

I will leave it for the experts to decide. For Momma to decide. For Ted to make some grand *pronunciamento*.

※

He'll make his decision within seconds, I should imagine. It wouldn't surprise me if he's still dining out on it in forty years' time. Yeah, he's certainly good for another forty or fifty. I can imagine him soft-chaired in his comfortable years, still pottering about with his bees when the new millennium dawns, still dribbling away about animals.

He'd be more moved more by the death of a fucking fox than my demise, I'll tell you.

You know Daddy was a world authority on bees. A world authority! He could hold one in his hand without being stung. How about that!

How did he do that, Momma? Did he never get stung?

Pop was an apiarist.

Husband a plagiarist.

Sylvia, what is she that all the swines commend her? A fatalist?

I always think there's something more than slightly asexual about writing about animals, don't you? Let me put my head on one side and consider it theatrically like Ted would do with his flaky head.

Let me give it some deep thought, Ted-style.

'Ah don't know, Sylv, Ah'm not at arl shewer!'

The only thing to write about for me, Ted, is *me*. How could I possibly write about anything else? I can only write about what I feel.

I think I could define poetry as what I feel about myself.

෴

There can't be long to go now. As nocturnal adventures go this is pretty much running out of steam and is in desperate need of some rising action. I figure we're long passed the introductory stages and are overdue the complication.

Let's stand up and pull back the curtains and see what we can see, while old night still clings to yon Heath of Hampstead hill. Most glorious night, thou wert not meant for slumber!

The old merciless moon again, making blue lizard scales of roof shingles ... and simple folk are bedded deep in eiderdown, sleeping soft and sound and ...

Oh my God, look at that! It isn't, is it? It wouldn't be ... a grey cat ... would it? No ... it's definitely white, I'm afraid. A white cat at night is one of the worst of bad luck omens, Ted would say.

Worse than spilling salt or stepping on a sidewalk crack, I think, but not as bad as cracking a mirror, maybe.

Aaaarrrggghhh!

I shouldn't have done that, I really shouldn't. Now there are bits of glass everywhere. Maybe I'll sweep them up later. Pretend it never happened. It was a mean old mirror anyway that never flattered me.

It's all nonsense, of course, all that divination mumbo. I've never understood how a man as intelligent as Ted went in for it all.

Let's close the curtains. I wish I'd never looked out. Why did I have to look out at that very moment? Isn't everything about moments?

Life is full of stretched seconds that will echo down the ages, long after … long after this long night has closed.

Shame on you, Sylvia, giving way like that to superstitious fears. It's at times like this that we find out most about ourselves and what we're made of.

Why should a woman as intelligent as I am have all these irrational demons, all this frenzy of resentment at everything, principally myself. I must be my own doctor, rehabilitate myself. No one else can cure me. I must get to bed and sleep it off. You're never going to sleep, sitting around here talking nonsense to yourself, Sylv. Just look at the time! You're going to be a real mess in the morning. Good for nothing!

※

I'd love to get away from here. I'd love to find peace again. Love to feel the sun again. I do not think I have had any peace since Daddy died. I mean why do people have to die? Why can't we all live happily ever after in Winkelburg with Momma Nix and Papa Nix?

This is Sylvia talking, the lost girl who never grew up and never will. I recognise her voice, know it well. She can get on my nerves at times. Can't someone tell her to shut up.

I may as well have the rest of these pills. No point saving them now.

Gee thanks, Dr. Horder.

Thanks for the popping pills, globoid jujubes candying my innards, hardening my resolve, dissolving my apoplexy, making me calm, very calm, before the storm.

I mean why do we have to die naturally? To die naturally is just plain unnatural, a waste of a life, a waste of a good death.

If we're all born to die, better to die on our own terms, at a time of our own choosing and by our own hand - *nicht wahr?*

My goodness, is that the four? I can't remember hearing the three. Maybe I did drift off. Or have I just miscounted? Not that it matters much. One hour is pretty much as good as the next at this juncture.

Dying is an art, like everything else. I do it exceptionally well.

I'm Sylvia and I've been praised as one of the greatest of our modern poets. I have everything to live for. I have two darling children sleeping peacefully in an adjacent room ... I do not have to die.

And ... a husband sleeping far from peacefully but full of his piece somewhere in darkest London. A croaky toad tooting in the night.

Destiny is in the air and I sit alone here in a house once owned by Yeats and in a room he must have known, contemplating ... going to the bathroom before ...

What was it Yeats said: 'The best lack all conviction, the worst are full of passionate intensity.' That's me, Sylvia, lacking all conviction and there's Ted, a man full of passionate intensity if ever there were one. So full of it does he imagine himself to be that he wants everybody to see it, be in awe of his genius for passionate intensity.

There was a time when the intensity of his passion for me knew no bounds.

I guess he has to keep on moving from one woman to another and always will do, the moment they've recognised him for what he is, warts and all - dandruff and all, should I say.

What will be said tomorrow, bruited abroad? Might the news spread up and down Fleet Street like wildfire? Will I make the evening editions?

Read all abart it! Read all abart it! Sylvia Plath tops herself!

Will my name ring down Piccadilly? Be spoken of in Covent Garden? Will my fame reach the shires? Will Cambridge mediocrities shake their heads and claim to have known me? There will be lively, colourful accounts, grizzly memories. She suffered a sort of mental breakdown, poor girl, the kinder folk will say.

Of course, they will all miss the point.

It will never be known how Babylon fell, though many will speculate.

What will Mr. H. actually do when he reads *all about it*? Will he sigh from that deep, deep soul of his and will he weep bitter tears? Will he shoulder some of the blame?

You bet he will not? Will he make poetical capital out of me? You bet your sweet life he will.

To hell with it! I will outlive the bastard. I will outlive them all! I will outlive him … even if … even if … even if it kills me!

You're laughing hysterically again, Sylv, old girl. You're going to have a seizure or something if you carry on like this.

If they remember him at all, the seborrhoea-flaked goofus, it will be because of me. Me!

Ring telephone ring! Make like the Inks Spots said. Go on, ring! Just ring! I dare you to! In this world of a billion people there must be someone out there who wants to speak to Sylvia, sweet Sylvia.

Okay, okay, it's the middle of the night, so the world sleeps. Only lunatics, lovers and poets avoid the common prejudice to sleep … to sleep deeply, peacefully, righteously. But you might expect God to ring, if He's watching.

Hello is there anybody there?

Are you there God?

Thought not!

You know when Daddy died I vowed never to speak to God again and I never have.

I was not even allowed to attend Daddy's funeral.

So, I am alone and unloved. Well, there's nothing new there. I like it best that way. Alone and unloved, maundering amongst the wastes, I can turn out a poem a day.

Let me catechise myself one last time? I always find it rather beneficial, part of the therapy.

Who am I? What am I? I am, above all, a poet. I can write. I have always been able to write. I had my first poem printed at the age of eight, you know. Eight! How about that! I was only eight and was a poet published in the *Boston Herald*! Mommy was proud, even though I had not made the twee little changes to my poem that she had suggested. She condescended me a smile and a pat on the back.

Maybe I should make a final entry in the journal ... for the sake of posterity. Calm yourself, Sylv, collect your thoughts, harvest them now. They are important.

I cannot, alas, write myself out of this black hole into which I seem to sink deeper and deeper? I can't think of a thing to set down.

I yearn for something that is not to be known. Yes, I suppose I could write down something on those lines. What do you yearn for, Sylvia!

I yearn for ... eternal peace.

Surely everybody is entitled to some peace, once in a while?

Why *should* I be beset with all these desperate, desperate thoughts? I have been sitting here like this night after night for weeks on end. So what's different tonight? In what respect are the atoms differing? Why this night of nights? What malign stars are in what malefic conflation?

※

'Every now and then there comes a time' - that's what it says here -'when the neutral and impersonal forces of the world turn and come together in a thunder-crack of judgement.'

Agreed! I understand perfectly, Sylvia. That makes sense to me.

I have felt like this before many times. Many times have I felt like this. That sounds better! Many times have I felt like this, felt so drawn to stare into the dark water and look at the fish but never quite so ... quite so fatalistically. Fatefully, I might say.

It's all a bloody mess.

I feel feverish, I need to walk, to pace about again. 'I'm walkin' the floor over you ... can't sleep a wink, but it's true ...'

I just love those old songs from the Forties that were playing all the time on the radio when I was a little girl. Who was it who sang it? Ernest Tubb! What a name! If I was called Ernest Tubb, I seriously think I'd change it to ... Clarence Tubb.

That's basically one of Ted's jokes. He'd laugh at that. This is certainly a night for laughing ... and crying and crying and laughing.

Who can say whether it is farce or tragedy, tragicomic or comically tragic? I never did care about literary terms and classifications and I am not going to start worrying my head about them now. Let the professorial types decide.

Maybe Prof Thomas will hear me if I tread heavily like this, bang about a bit, and will come up. Maybe he will knock on the door and I will not answer him. What if he won't take no for an answer? Maybe he'll batter the door down.

I wonder if he will.

It's not really in my control, is it? If I were relying on Prof Thomas for my salvation, I wouldn't rate my chances as very high. Pity I don't possess a Smith and Weston just so I could make assurance doubly sure.

Would I still feel like this if Ted was here? If Ted *were* here I should say! We're in England, best to use the subjunctive. You never know who's listening!

If Ted had always been here with me instead of elsewhere in his thoughts and in his body? Is it something within me trying to force itself out - or something outside of me trying to force itself into my innermost being? That is the question.

When I was a little girl ... I used to think I would never die. The young never contemplate it, do they?

They think they'll live forever. Forever and ever, Amen. Amen. Ah men! Men. Sons of Adam, born of Eve.

Eve? Nay, 'tis morn. The clock has already struck four.

Was that a yawn, the first yawn of morn? I do believe I begin to feel drowsy. A drowsy numbness pains my sense as though of hemlock I had drunk.

Who was it who said that? It certainly wasn't me - or Ted!

It would not greatly surprise me if I were to fall asleep now and wake up later with the light streaming through the curtains, my heartache and *calentura* gone. It's happened before, you know. It happens a lot.

Generally, I feel better the next day, like Andromeda unchained.

※

What *is* the new day going to make of it all? What will be said, whispered close in literary ears about the mad American? Will they quote her lines – quote them against her? Will she be read more posthumously than when alive? A poet's reputation, a poet's essential worth, never really begins, does it, until a line can be drawn under her lines.

Then the creepy scholars take over, the flesh flies hovering and hoovering about the corpse, establishing the *oeuvre*. The *oeuvre*! That's a word to savour. Plath's '*oeuvre.*'

I can hear them intoning it in their colleges, all those stooping tweedy men in milk bottle glasses and those salivating blue stockings who have never written a line in their lives. Patiently assembling it, line by line, for other critics to pick over and later critics to pick over again ... and again and again... until the end of time.

Or do I fool myself? In all probability I will be sitting in this seat tomorrow, having the same damn thoughts - damned thoughts indeed - having the same demons pouting and posturing the same pouts and postures at me, like grinning gargoyles, holding the same conversations with myself.

Life goes on. Life goes on. It generally goes on, so contrives it, manages it somehow. People endure down the years. Except Daddy. Daddy did not endure. He was pushed beyond endurance. Papa, my beautiful Papa.

As a little girl, I used to think ... indeed, I firmly believed ... that he would always be with me. He and I would live forever ... and forever amen. Maybe Papa was the only man I ever really loved.

I was ten when they buried you ...
At twenty I tried to die ...
And get back, back, back to you ...
I thought even the bones would do ...
But they pulled me out of the sack ...
And they stuck me together with glue ...
And then I knew what to do ...
I made a model of you ...

A man in black with a Meinkampf look …
And a love of the rack and the screw …
And I said I do, I do.
I think I'm over him now.
And yet! And yet!

I remember his smell, a good manly smell. He didn't have dandruff! The strength of his arms. His grip, firm but tender. Does every girl secretly love her father more than her lover? I might have written a poem on that. I might have written a volume. I might … I might, if I were not hell-bent on leaving early.

He didn't have dandruff, no, not my *alles in ordnung* German Daddy. He just had gangrene, rising grey and green and pestilential, in his leg. That's all!

Yes, go ahead and cry, Sylvia, let the tears flow. You'll feel better for it. It has been a night for tears.

And he ignored it. The stupid, stupid, brave, cowardly man just ignored it. Let it bubble and blossom like chemical damp … devouring him, pestilentially. Stinking to high heaven.

Meesa Masheena!

Oh my God! Do not think on it, Sylvia.

As suicides go that would be the worst kind. That would be too cruel. Too cruel to those he left behind.

Wie absolut blutigen schrecklich!

How does that cute little song go? Let me try to sing it, like a little girl might sing it to her papa.

'Oh, my papa, to me he was so wonderful
Oh, my papa, to me he was so good;
No one could be, so gentle and so lovable,
Oh, my papa, he always understood.

Gone are the days when he could take me on his knee
And with a smile he'd change my tears to laughter.

Oh, my papa, so funny, so adorable,
Always the clown so funny in his way
Oh, my papa, to me he was so wonderful
Deep in my heart ... I miss him so today.'

I couldn't write like that. I sometimes wish I could have. How wonderful to have simplistic thoughts like that. Sometimes I wonder whether it's better to touch the heart of millions with a corny old song than to write true poetry that ordinary people do not understand - and weedy, tweedy doctors of philosophy and spindle-shanked spinsters think they do ... and undoubtedly do not.

Why did you abandon me, oh my father, put me in bed with my mother!

Daddy?

What was it Richard wrote? I was shocked when I read it. It was the sort of thing to bring a blush to a young girl's cheeks.

I *am* shocked when I remember it now. Well only a little.

'I am talking myself into thinking it will be rather fun to play daddy to a naughty girl if you are naughty.'

Naughty? That was an understatement, Mr. Sassoon, Yale scholar - same blood as Wilfred Owen's friend - and my greatest love?

Probably, my greatest love.

I remember one Saturday, in Spring, when New York was utterly wondrously beautiful and the park was blooming and the air was spinning and my heart was falling in love. Walking down 44th Street, holding hands with you, Richard, naughty heart pumping, looking for our naughty hotel, where we could be naughty all night long. And we were. Boy, were we ever! Naughty, naughty, naughty! My heart shouts with joy at the memory of it.

Hell, we were not naughty at all. Naught was naughty that we did. We were pure and innocent. Idealistic to a fault, maybe, and loving ...

You were hardly my idea of big hunky boy, Richard, no lantern jaw and boulders for shoulders for you, but I did love you. Did you ever love me? I mean in your heart.

But we sure had a lotta fun, didn't we just.

Say, do you remember that time ice-skating at the Rockefeller, the big tree all brassily, sassily Chrismassy, and the whole of the city ablaze with lights. Oysters for breakfast, snails for dinner. Didn't we just think ourselves a couple of swells. 'We're a couple of swells,' we sang as we strutted down Fifth Avenue, Christmas-shopping without actually stopping to try or buy, just happy to be with each other.

Dear Richard, when I think of you I always think of Christmas, somehow. We had two of them. We were students. I was in Cambridge, you were in Paris. Just grab a train you said, come and spend Christmas in Paris, I'll show you around.

Two Americans in Paris, wide-eyed innocent lovers. Let's lose ourselves in the city of freedom, you said – yet everywhere we went, we could never escape *La Tour D' Eiffel*. It was always there like some great looming presence. We were under it, or over it or next to it. You can never get lost in Paris with that thing always in the offing, gathering its greatness everywhere, night and day.

You wanted to show me the sights. Your eyes sparkled with boyish excitement at every new thing. We walked up the *Champs-Élysées* and just stood there, holding hands, trying to take it all in. We sipped hot chocolate in *Les Deux Magots* and you quoted Victor Hugo.

You would keep pointing to all these *Belle Époque* buildings with literary associations but d'you know what I remember best, Richard? I remember *Place Pigalle* and the prostitutes, the 'hordes of broads' you called them, standing around in all their cheap and gaudy finery.

They were far from drab!

You know in some ways I almost envied them their simple bookless existence. God it must be so easy if the most difficult thing you ever have to do is to strap on a garter-belt and get yourself … you know, Richard.

Where is it? What was it I wrote? Ah yes here it is. Let me devour it.

Yes, that's right, we went to Nice on New Year's Day, didn't we? When I saw that red sun rising like the eyes of God out of that screaming blue sea, I did not want to go back to the grey roofs and greyer skies of grey as gooseflesh Cambridge ever again. That was my most urgent thought at the time, which came upon me like a revelation.

Cambridge I had done with, and yet I went back.

There was another time in Paris. A fell time! An Easter.

I came to you and you were not there. I feel chilled to the bone to recall it. While I walked the streets looking for you, looking for someone, anyone, before skulking back home again like some forlorn and forgotten creature, you were sunning yourself in Spain. In fucking Spain you were doing the fucking samba!

The Gods were mocking me, I know it. I was sitting

in some room belonging to that kindly old concierge who'd taken pity on me. I was, indeed, a piteous figure - even her poodle patted me with his paw - writing a letter to you, crying bitter, bitter tears and what came on the radio in French but 'Smile while your heart is breaking'.

I mean ... what more can be said?

It was some Passover! *Chag kashruth pesach.*

You lost me then, Richard, in that moment - and, in a way, Ted found me.

If only life could always be put in a nutshell like that - but the truth is seldom that easy to see.

༒

There was another Richard, you know, way back: Richard Norton.

I put that Richard in my book, Richard. I called him Buddy Willard. There, the secret's out! I can rest easy now. But Mommy must never know.

I'm feeling old and cold and I'm getting bored with myself. I think it's about time, anyway.

I must confess the condemned woman could do with a last smoke, if one were available, which it isn't, so we'll have to do without.

Anyway, as Ted says, they're bad for my health. Gallows' humour again, Sylv. You're not supposed to be the one laughing.

It's time to go to bed. It's getting late, so late it will soon be early, as Shakespeare might have said. As Shakespeare would have said, indeed could not help himself saying.

I must look in on the children, fix them some bread and milk for the morning. Let me tidy away a few things and rule off the journal.

That's finished, anyway. Homework done. That would have pleased Momma. Although … she would have rebuked me for not sweeping up the broken glass.

But I don't want to cut myself. I might bleed.

I remember, Momma, you always piled your hair up on your head … to make yourself a few inches taller, didn't you! That's one of the things that's just popped into my mind, I don't know why.

※

Sleeping soundly the pair of them. I can't bear to look at them. I can't bear to. What if they should wake up now?

Let me kiss you both goodbye, very gently so not to disturb you.

Goodbye, dear children, think of Momma now and then and never bad thoughts.

To look at them, flesh of my flesh, bone of my bone, is to break my heart. To look at innocence before committing a crime, a crime against their very nature, is something I cannot do.

Promise me, Ted, that you will take them away to a

better place and be a good father to them. If you can promise me this I will resign them to you now and face death unflinchingly.

Do this one last thing for me, Ted. For both of us. For our family.

'But, Sylv, Ah've got *obligations* elsewhere.'

Ted, I'm begging you, on my hands and knees. These tears I shed are sacred tears of blood.

'But, Sylv, let's not do anything hasty.'

It's something I must do and shall. Think of Frieda and little Nicholas, Ted. What kind of life would they have brought up by a mother like me? Your *obligations* are to them, Ted. Do this one last thing for me, Ted, for the memory of what we once were to each other.

'If you're sure it's something you really want, Sylv.'

Certain sure, Ted.

'I guess it's all for the best, then, really.'

It is, Ted. It is!

༄

Really, really it is. I'm almost certain it is.

There you go again, Sylv, lacking conviction, even at these decisive moments.

Of course, I can't be certain … no one can ever be certain about anything.

Except Ted. Ted is always certain about something … or someone.

Ted is abed now, probably scratching his head as he fornicates in his dreams. Even asleep he'll be making certain.

Time for me to go to bed too ... to sleep ... perchance to dream ... in the kitchen with the gas hissing. I hope I put a shilling in the meter last night. That would be the final bitterest of ironies, wouldn't it!

'Stop laughing, Sylvia. You can't have fits of hysterics at a moment like this. It's not seemly. Not dignified. It's making a mockery of things.'

Sorry, I'll try.

'You'll wake the kids. Get a grip on yourself.'

Sorry, Mommy.

This is your last chance to ring, phone! Paging Mr. Telephone! Final call for Mr. Telephone!

No! Not even a tiny tinny little tinkle, you mute inglorious thing.

Could there, in this great big world, be anybody out there like me, waiting in this desperate moment for their phone to ring? I wonder. If there is, we could kinda hook up together?

Are you there, buddy!

There's nobody there, Ted.

No?

All I can hear is my own heart.

Let me take a deep breath and listen one last time to the old brag of my heart. De-dum, de-dum, de-dum - I am, I am, I am.

There it goes! There it goes! There it goes! A summoning gong.

I don't think it's ever beat like this before, so strong and insistent and loud, like an alarm clock about to go off. Like a ticking time-bomb.

There's not much wrong with a heart that can beat like that.

You know, old friend, after thirty years, I am none the wiser about what makes you beat and what each beat signifies. Too late to ask if end were worth the means. Let us pull down the curtain, let down the veil, the veil, the veil! Life's been to no avail, it seems.

We have come so far … We can go no further.

Let me have one final lingering look around the room that has held me captive. It's not much to cry over, Sylv. You're not missing much.

※

The moment one definitely commits oneself, the way becomes plain.

And so to the kitchen, always my least favourite room in any house.

The first and last resort of the lonely housewife. The perfect stage for a woman's act of desperation, her final solution.

They will be haunted and assailed and puzzled, no doubt, by the ending. But the message is simple and serene. The yearning for perfection is not unattainable though it can only be achieved in death.

It hisses like a snake, waits for the match that does not come, hisses some more. It is a drowsy hiss. A not unpleasant hiss.

Its snaky acids hiss. It petrifies the will. These are the isolate, slow faults that kill, that kill, that kill …

This is how it would have been for them, Daddy, in the gas chambers.

We did not avoid our fate, after all …

No one ever does.

Epilogue

Sylvia Plath's death by her own hand, at the age of thirty, was not the end but, perhaps, the beginning of something resembling a Greek tragedy. Sylvia might well be cast as the archetypal tragic literary heroine, the female poet in mental turmoil, the betrayed woman - blonde to boot - and questions asked darkly about the curse on the generations.

Sadly, her son, Nicholas Hughes, who did not learn of the manner of his mother's death until he was a teenager, was also to take his own life, in March, 2009, at the age of 47. A professor of fisheries and ocean sciences, he hung himself having battled depression for many years. He was not married and had no children, and apparently did his best to avoid discussing his parents and their literary associations, spending most of his time in deepest Alaska.

Several biographers have blamed Ted Hughes for bringing about the split with Sylvia by having an affair with Assia Wevill, the wife of fellow poet, David Wevill. Assia herself seems unwittingly drawn into a catalogue of misadventure, having been pregnant with Ted's baby when Sylvia Plath killed herself, but having the baby aborted.

After Sylvia died, by all accounts Assia stepped into Sylvia's position, for a time looking after the two children. Tragedy struck again, in March 1969, when aged 42 and in a state of deep depression, she murdered the couple's four-year-old daughter, Alexandra Tatiana Elise, known fondly as Shura, before taking her own life - in the kitchen of her flat in Clapham, in circumstances not dissimilar from those attending Sylvia's death. The major difference is that, instead of protecting her child, she administered sleeping tablets dissolved in water to Shura and to herself, before turning on the gas oven. It seemed she feared to leave her child alive, believing Ted had never offered her true acceptance or love.

Ted, both as the keeper of Sylvia Plath's legacy as well as father of her children, is inextricably bound up in the tragedy, if that is what we are calling it. He was made Poet Laureate in 1984 and died on 28th October, 1998, aged 68. His last work, *Birthday Letters,* released only a month before his death, throws some light on his personal feelings towards Sylvia's death. They do not appear to be of unmixed sorrow or affection. One poem *18 Rugby Street*, about the house where they spent their wedding night, records their first sexual encounter in no very flattering terms, describing Sylvia as a 'great bird of prey' surging 'in the plumage of your excitement'. He refers to her 'roundy face, that your friends, being objective, called "rubbery"', and her nose as 'broad and Apache, nearly a boxer's nose'. Woundingly, he appends the lines: 'Scorpio's obverse to the semitic eagle / That made every camera your enemy' and, ungallantly, draws attention to a facial scar 'like a Maker's flaw'. Such writing has hardly endeared him to those who admire Sylvia, or absolved him of culpability. As if drawn to the idea of the Greek tragedy, Hughes appears to suggest in *The Shot*, and elsewhere, that Sylvia had an Electra Complex, being unnaturally in love with her father, Otto, who died, in 1940, when she was eight - when complications arose after his leg had been amputated.

Aurelia Plath, who in 1975 published her daughter's letters from 1950 to 1963 as *Letters Home*, alone lived to a ripe old age, dying peacefully, aged 87, in March 1994.

Frieda Hughes, born in April 1960, was almost three at the time of her mother's death. A poet and painter of some reputation, she became an Australian citizen in 1992 and continues to live on that continent.

Printed in Great Britain
by Amazon